To Gay Bell
and South Hill Tots

You have truly been
a ray of golden
sunshine in our lives.

Love,

KIERAN

KC, Jude and Chow Mein

FOR RENT

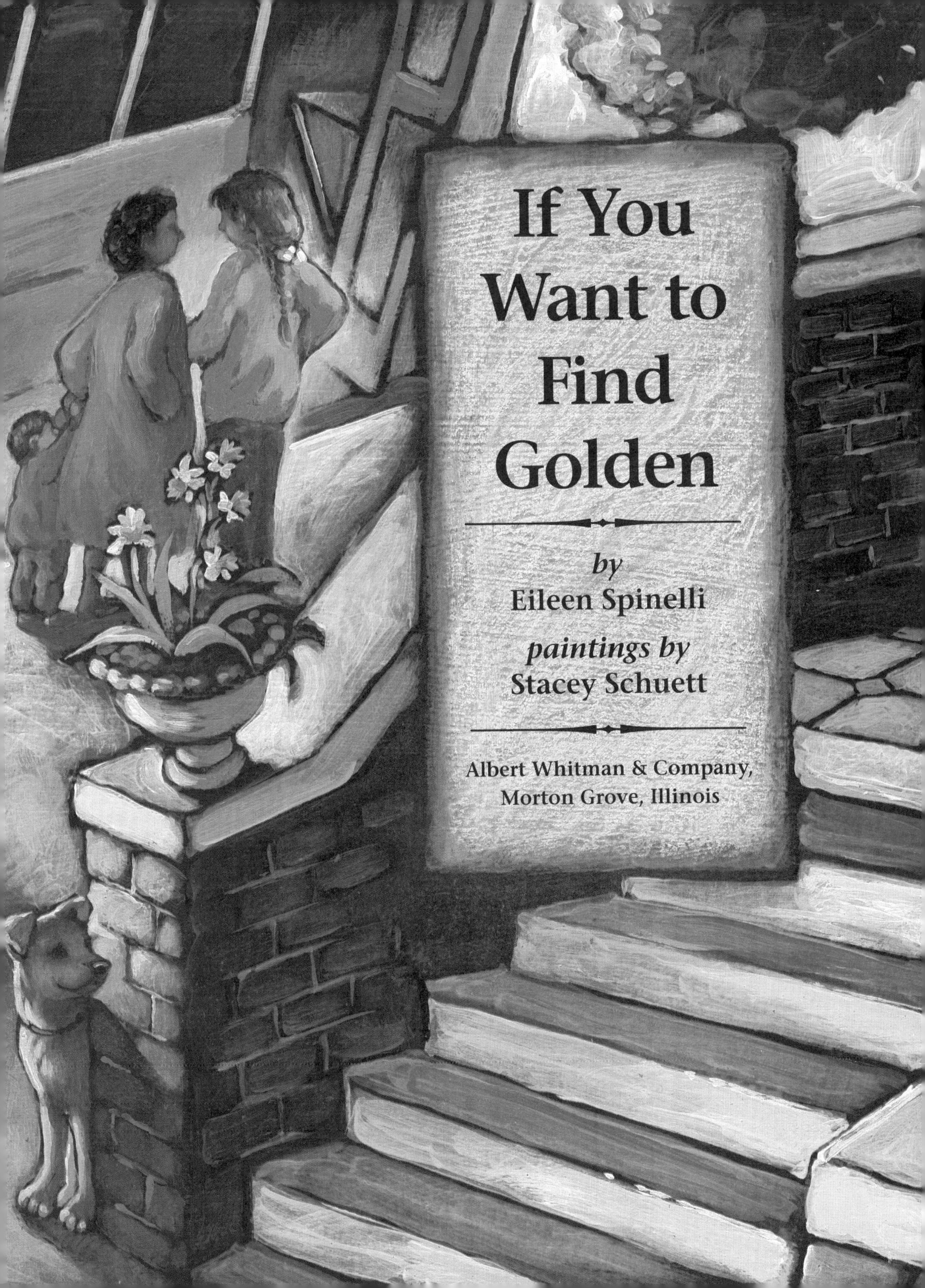

If You Want to Find Golden

by
Eileen Spinelli
paintings by
Stacey Schuett

Albert Whitman & Company,
Morton Grove, Illinois

Published in 1993 by Albert Whitman & Company,
6340 Oakton Street, Morton Grove, Illinois 60053-2723.
Published simultaneously in Canada by
General Publishing, Limited, Toronto.

Printed in the United States of America.
10 9 8 7 6 5 4 3 2 1

Designer: Sandy Newell.
Text typeface: Stone Serif.
Illustration media: Acrylic and pastel.

Library of Congress Cataloging-in-Publication Data
Spinelli, Eileen.
If you want to find golden / Eileen Spinelli ;
illustrated by Stacey Schuett.
p. cm.
Summary: A trip through the city streets brings contact with many colors, from an orange construction sign to gray pigeons.
ISBN 0-8075-3585-0
[1. Color–Fiction. 2. City and town life–Fiction.]
I. Schuett, Stacey, ill. II. Title.
PZ7.S7566If 1993
[E]–dc20
93-12000
CIP
AC

For Patty Beaumont, Nick McKenna,
and Mary Anita Kentz,
golden all. E.S.

For Lesly.
S.S.

If you want to find golden,
watch the morningrise melt
across rooftops
and splash against windows.
There's a man on the street corner
who plays golden saxophone.
Listen to the music,
dance in the sun,
if you want to find golden.

125

Special

If you want to find white,
stop by the diner
where a waiter in a white apron
will serve you milk
and a sugary cream doughnut.
There are paper napkins
for spills and smudges.
You can chat with the chef
in her tall hat
or peek at the meringue pies
in the case,
if you want to find white.

If you want to find green,
there's a traffic light.
It says *go*!
Go to the greengrocer's,
smell the green onions,
browse about the racks
of lettuce and spinach,
nibble on a sprig of cilantro,
if you want to find green.

STOP

If you want to find orange,
look for the "Men at Work" sign.
There will be orange cones
and orange vests.
You can feel the heat
of the flame in the barrel
as the workers keep warm.
You can pet
the patchy marmalade cat nearby,
if you want to find orange.

If you want to find blue,
look up,
sing a joyful, skyful song.
Wave to the policewoman
and the boy on the blue bike.
There are bright sparks
flying from a jackhammer–
keep your distance!
You can drop a letter
in the corner mailbox,
if you want to find blue.

PA

If you want to find yellow,
there are taxis
zipping down the street
and a school bus stopped
to pick up children.
There's a street vendor
selling hot dogs.
You can squirt
thick, yellow mustard,
wave away a pesky bee,
if you want to find yellow.

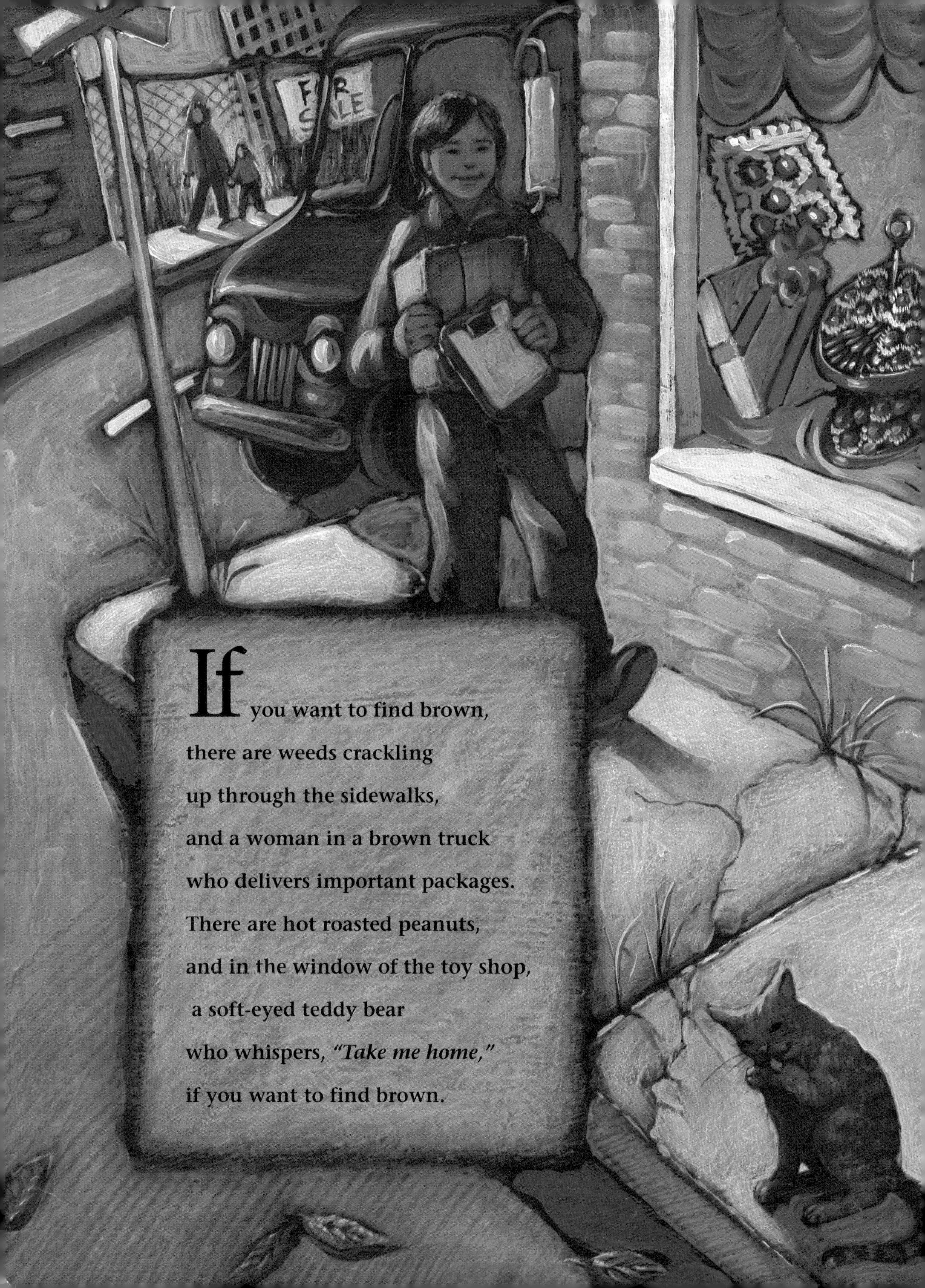

If you want to find brown,
there are weeds crackling
up through the sidewalks,
and a woman in a brown truck
who delivers important packages.
There are hot roasted peanuts,
and in the window of the toy shop,
a soft-eyed teddy bear
who whispers, *"Take me home,"*
if you want to find brown.

HALL'S
Chocolates

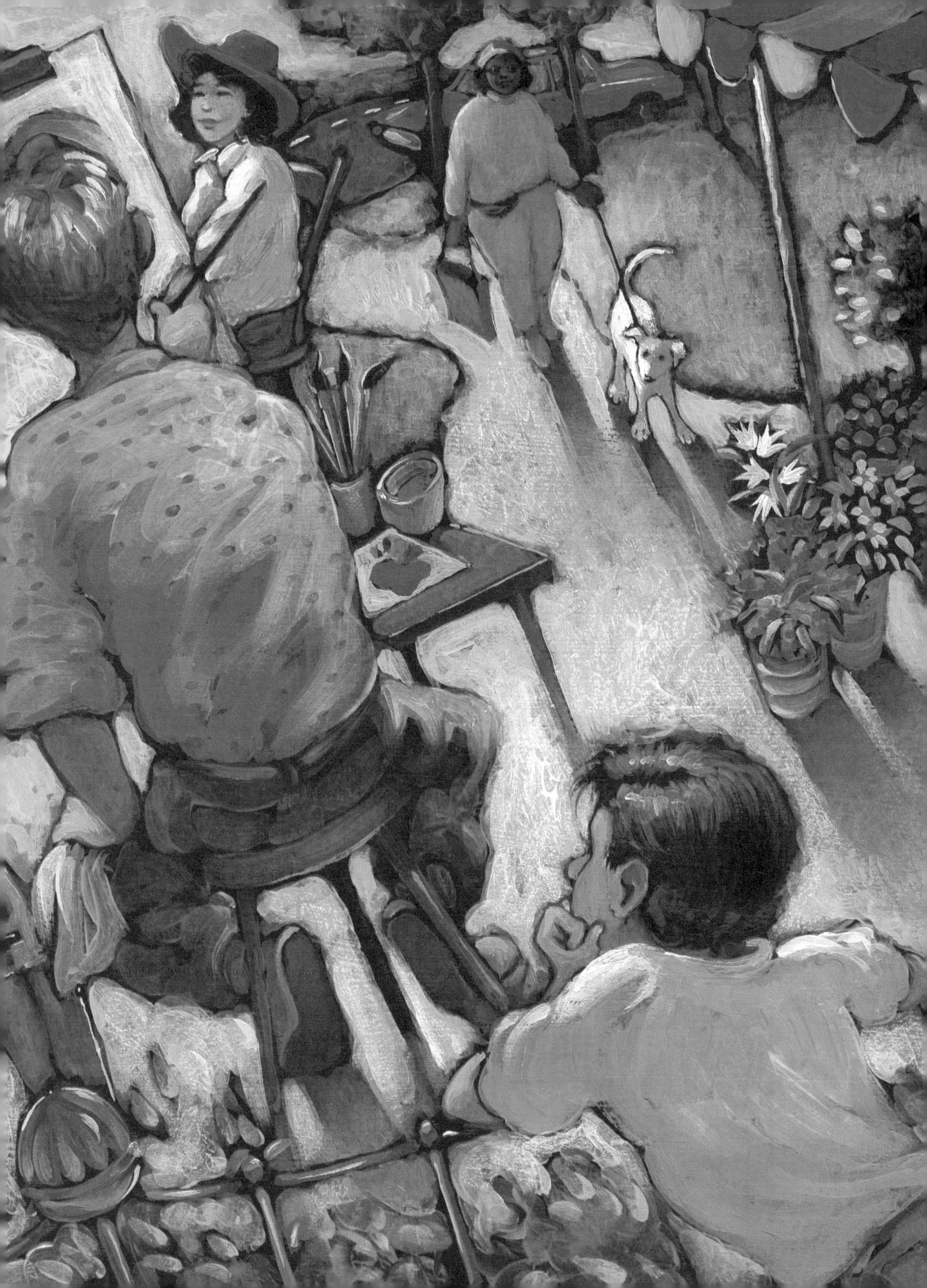

If you want to find purple,
there are violets
in the florist's shop
to remind you it's spring,
and plump purple grapes
at the fruit stand.
The street artist paints
a girl in a purple hat.
You can watch how he does it,
if you want to find purple.

If you want to find gray,
you can count the pigeons
in the courthouse eaves
or play peek-a-boo
with stately statues.
You can splash in
old stone fountains,
study skyscrapers
and steamy curls of chimney smoke,
if you want to find gray.

If you want to find red,
look out!
Here comes a fire engine
clanging uptown.
When your ears stop ringing,
there's a tugboat
slow-going downriver
and a red balloon floating
just beyond your fingertips.
You can try to catch it,
if you want to find red.

If you want to find copper,
surprise!
There's a penny on the pavement.
You can toss that rusted can
into the trash bin
(no litterbug, you),
and say goodbye to the afternoon
as sunset burnishes
the beams of buildings,
if you want to find copper.

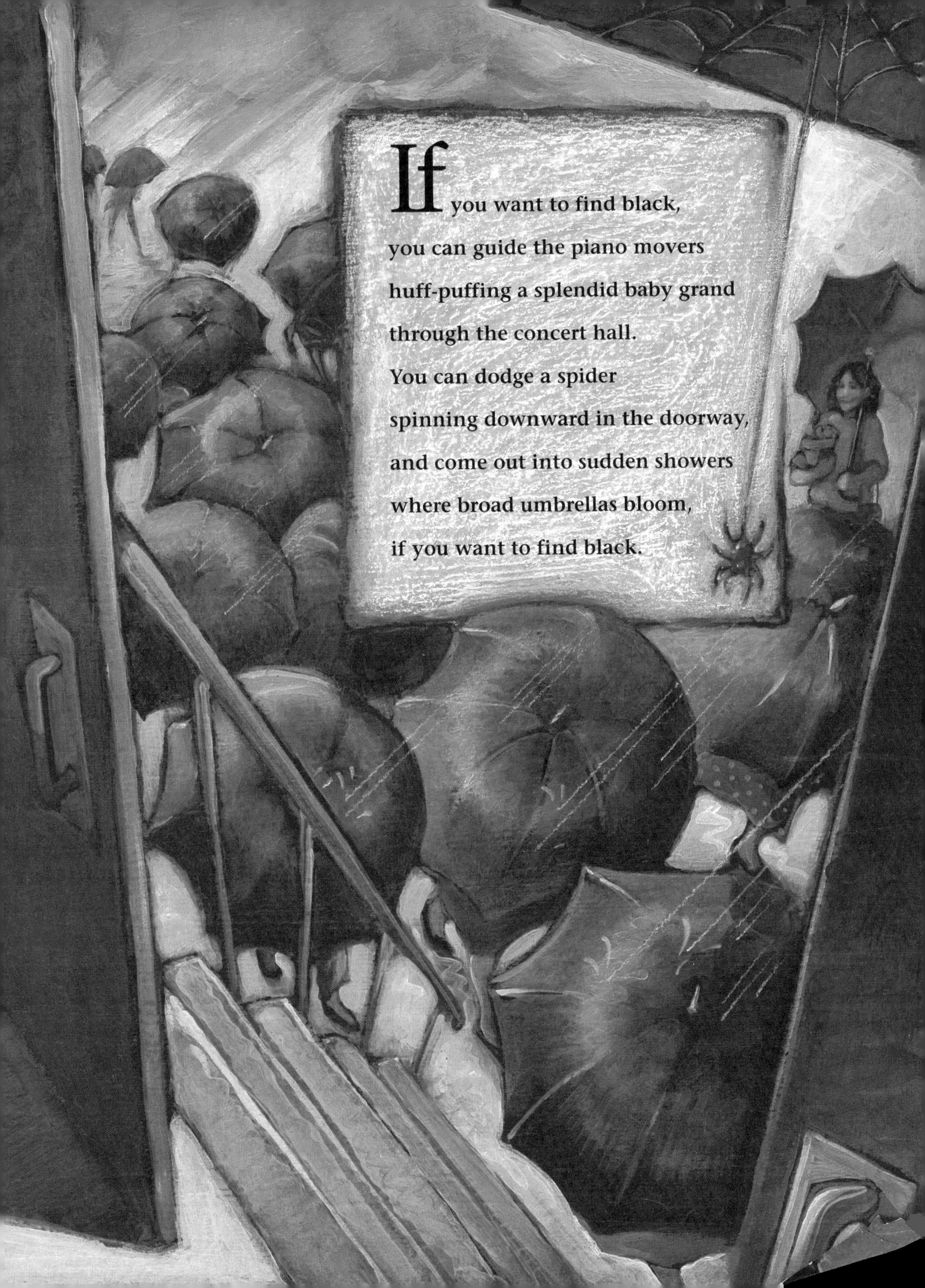

If you want to find black,
you can guide the piano movers
huff-puffing a splendid baby grand
through the concert hall.
You can dodge a spider
spinning downward in the doorway,
and come out into sudden showers
where broad umbrellas bloom,
if you want to find black.

If you want to find silver,
you can stay out till dark
when all the lights go on,
and the city is spattered with stars.
You can touch a wisp of shimmery dress
as the singer rushes into the theater.
You can go home, climb into bed,
listen to the silver tinkling party sounds
of the city as you fall asleep,
if you want to find silver.

Sweet Dreams!

FOR
RENT